FOR MARKOSIA ENTERPRISES LTD

HARRY MARKOS
Publisher & Managing Partner

IAN SHARMAN · GM JORDAN · TOBY SHORT
Group Editors

ANDY BRIGGS
Creative Consultant

Chapter one:
The Dreamer

"A WORLD SO HARD AND BRIGHT LIKE GOLDEN SEAM...

...PERCHANCE A STAGE-CRAFT TRICK, A SLEEPER'S DREAM"

"IS STINKING DUNG NOT PROOF OF WAKEFULNESS AND LIGHT?"

"OR MERE FANTAS'M OF THE MIND IN DEEPES OF NIGHT"

"IF ALL IS DREAM WHO THEN CALL I MOTHER?"

"OR AM I THE DREAMING OF ANOTHER?"

MORE? BUT THE BATTLE IS SURELY *WON.* WHO *ELSE* SURVIVES?

I AM VICTORIOUS AND WORN AND WEARY BEYOND DESCRIPTION.

THE VICTOR? YOU'VE WON A *SKIRMISH* NO MORE.

HOURS FROM NOW- IN *HELLISH DISPAIR* - YOU WILL THINK YOU WERE LIVELY AT THIS MOMENT AS A GAMBOLING LAMB.

NEVERTHELESS, I WILL GIVE YOU *RESPITE.*

A COMPANION. A BODYGUARD. A ROCK TO LEAN ON.

A BREATH!

A HEARTBEAT!

A FLICKER OF CONCIOUSNESS -- THE EXPECTANT WEIGHT OF A WOMB.

I LIVE!

SHE WILL PROTECT YOU FOR LONG ENOUGH TO DO WHAT YOU MUST.

WAIT - DO WHAT? WHAT *MORE* MUST I DO?

FARE THEE WELL.

BEFORE I REST I HAVE ONE MORE PLACE TO VISIT.

WRONG ON BOTH COUNTS. SEE HERE A WARRANT FOR MY ARREST.

SAYS MARLOWE IS A *HERETIC*. THEY WOULD SEE ME IN *THE TOWER*. BROKEN ON THE RACK AND HEADLESS WITHIN THE WEEK!

Arrest Warrant

For the apprehension of traitor, heretic and sodomist

Christopher Marlowe.

The holder of this warrant hereby enjoins the publick to offer all assistance and intelligence on his whereabouts.

Reward offered.

Dated in the year of the Lord 29th May 1593.

God save the Queen.

IN GODS NAME FLY, LEAVE THE CITY, A BOAT TO ROTTERDAM!

IN GOD'S NAME? IF THERE IS NO GOD THEN RETRIBUTION CANNOT BE FEARED!

ALL OF US, QUEEN AND COMMONER WILL BE TRAMPLED BY TIME'S GALLOPING STEED.

AND AS FOR THE WARRANT - MARLOWE PISSES ON IT!

CAN YOU HEAR THAT?

HEAR WHAT?

THAT *HUM*. AS IF THE WALL HARBOURED A WASPS NEST.

MICE PERCHANCE BUT *NOT* WASPS.

NAY - CLOSER STILL. LIKE A *BANSHEE* WAKING INSIDE MY VERY SKULL!

TOO LOUD!

MY SKULL... SHALL BURST!

AND IT BURNS WHITE FLAME!

HELP ME!

HELP ME-E-E!

CHRISTOPHER MARLOWE. I HAVE COME FOR YOU FROM FAR AWAY.

CHRIST'S BOLLOCKS!! BLOODY PISS AND COCKSHIT!

HUH?

UNBELIEVEABLE - HE FOLLOWED MY SIGNAL BACK TO THE SOURCE!

WHAT DO WE DO?

DO? WE STAY CLEAR. WE DON'T ALARM HIM. HE'S FRIGHTENED. DISORIENTATED. IN SHOCK.

BRING SOME CLOTHES. GET A MEDIC IN TO SEE TO HIS BLEEDING.

CHRISTOPHER. KIT. LISTEN TO ME. MY NAME IS WALSINGHAM. HELEN WALSINGHAM.

DOES THAT NAME MEAN ANYTHING TO YOU?

WALSINGHAM?! FRANCIS WALSINGHAM'S DAUGHTER?

ER - NOT QUITE.

COULD WE HAVE SOME LIGHT IN HERE?

Constantinople -
Dawn, 29th May 1453

"the siren-called noble holds his faith true and fair"

"Constantine kneels erect 'mongst nuns and solemn priests"

"thus do Byzantium's last defenders gather"

"the ruler's noble gaze sets free mens' hearts aflame"

"the cannon from his dreams trains its pitiless eye and prepares to ravish the city's rotting breast"

"the great sultan Mehmet, a hawk above the prey, swoops on sleeping babe. fire burns in his chest."

from "Byzantium vanquished" by Sir Thomas Mallory

CONSTANTINOPLE FALLS.
AND THE WESTWARD EXODUS OF ARTISTS AND PHILOSOPHERS CREATES THE RENAISSANCE.
YOU DO WELL MALLORY, BUT NOW WE DISCUSS WEIGHTIER MATTERS.
NIETZSCHE? HERE NOW? WHEREFORE?
I SUMMON THE WAR COUNCIL, MALLORY.
FOR I FEAR THE NEXT CITADEL TO FALL MAY BE OURS.

I count religion but a childish toy,
And hold there is no sin but ignorance.

Christopher Marlowe

Chapter two:
The Dragon

MONSTERS SEPARATED FROM ME BEHIND A FLIMSY GLASS WINDOW.

CHOKING FUME FROM TITANIC MANUFACTURIES CHANGES THE VERY WEATHER.

AND SILVER VESSELS PROJECT MULTITUDES ACROSS THE HEAVENS.

SO BE IT.

AMAZEMENT SIGNALS FAILURE OF THE IMAGINATION. AND MARLOWE LACKS NOT IMAGINATION.

AND YET - ONE REVELATION ROBS THE SPEECH FROM MY THROAT --

WILLIAM SHAKESPEARE, IMBECILE, HACK, COPYIST AND ARSE-HARLOT - NOW LAUDED AS THE WORLD'S GREATEST PLAYWRIGHT?

LET'S NOT GO THERE RIGHT NOW, YEAH?

THERE'S A BUNCH OF OTHER ISSUES I WANT TO TOUCH BASE ABOUT.

'TOUCH BASE' 'ISSUES' ?

YEAH, YOU KNOW - LIKE WHAT DO YOU KNOW ABOUT THE BARDS OF NEMETON?

AND WHY DID THEY TRY TO KILL YOU?

AND HOW DID YOU FOLLOW ME?

AH, THOSE ISSUES. LET'S SEE -

MY LAST MEAL WAS HALF A THOUSAND YEARS AGO.

MY LAST ACT WAS TO CUT A FAERIE IN HALF.

A WINGED HARPIE ALMOST DRILLED A KNIFE THROUGH MY SKULL.

AND YOU WANT TO DISCUSS 'ISSUES'!?

OK - CHILL YEAH?

YOU NEED TO BREATH SOME NEGATIVE IONS INTO THOSE ELIZABETHAN LUNGS OF YOURS.

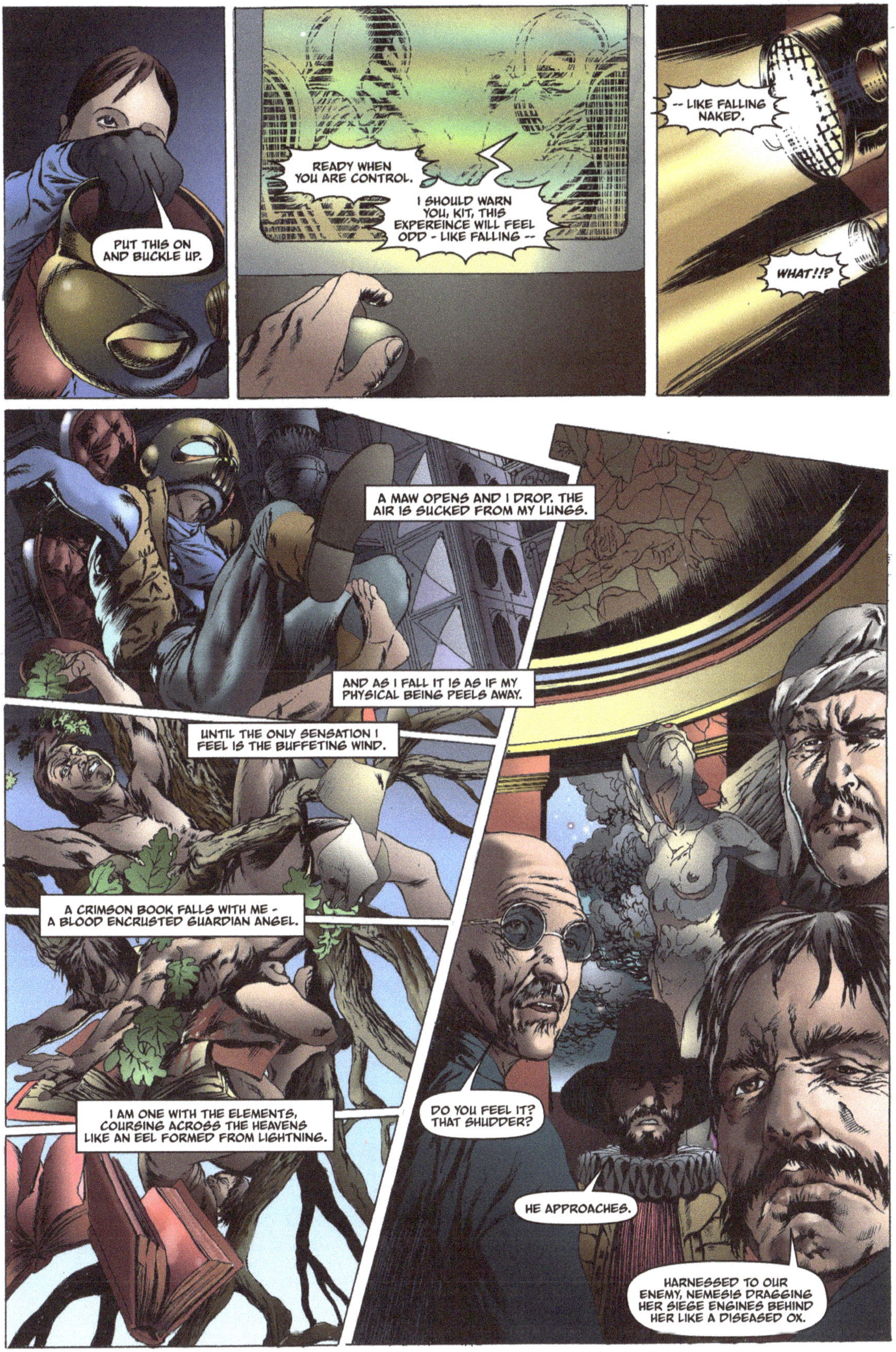

PUT THIS ON AND BUCKLE UP.

READY WHEN YOU ARE CONTROL.

I SHOULD WARN YOU, KIT, THIS EXPEREINCE WILL FEEL ODD - LIKE FALLING --

-- LIKE FALLING NAKED.

WHAT!!?

A MAW OPENS AND I DROP. THE AIR IS SUCKED FROM MY LUNGS.

AND AS I FALL IT IS AS IF MY PHYSICAL BEING PEELS AWAY.

UNTIL THE ONLY SENSATION I FEEL IS THE BUFFETING WIND.

A CRIMSON BOOK FALLS WITH ME - A BLOOD ENCRUSTED GUARDIAN ANGEL.

I AM ONE WITH THE ELEMENTS, COURSING ACROSS THE HEAVENS LIKE AN EEL FORMED FROM LIGHTNING.

DO YOU FEEL IT? THAT SHUDDER?

HE APPROACHES.

HARNESSED TO OUR ENEMY, NEMESIS DRAGGING HER SIEGE ENGINES BEHIND HER LIKE A DISEASED OX.

THEN OUT OF THE WIND COMES LIGHT --

AN OMPHALOS – GATEWAY TO THE UNDERWORLD – A CONFLUENCE OF GREAT LEY POWER.

WE'RE ABOVE THE SITE OF WHAT WILL, 5,000 YEARS FROM NOW, BE PRAGUE CASTLE.

NOT DREAMS - MADNESS! SKULLFUCKING, BRANDY-ADDLED MADNESS!

CONCENTRATE, MARLOWE. YOU WANT TO UNDERSTAND, YEAH?

LOOK, THE WALLS OF THE PIT. THE CHALK FIGURES ETCHED THERE. DO YOU SEE?

I – I DO AND HOW PASSING STRANGE... THEY SEEM FAMILIAR, LIKE AN ECHO OF MEMORY.

DAMN! I THINK OUR ARRIVAL HAS SPOOKED THE PRIESTS.

THE SPEAR! BEWARE! BEWARE!

RELAX, WHAT YOU SEE OF ME IS SIMPLY A DIGITAL PROJECTION OF THE EGO.

OUR REAL SELVES ARE SAFE IN THE LAB.

LET'S FOCUS ON OUR PURPOSE FOR BEING HERE.

LOOK AT THESE SYMBOLS

WHEREVER WE GO – AND WHENEVER – NO MATTER HOW ISOLATED THE LOCATION, WE'LL FIND THE SAME MOTIFS.

I FEEL I DO KNOW THEM - SIGNS GLIMPSED UNFATHOMLY IN THE MIND'S DEEP.

THIS STONE CIRCLE IS SACRED TO THE DRUIDS, A *NEMETON*.

LOOK THERE - A SACRIFICIAL CEREMONY. THE VICTIM GOING WILLINGLY TO HIS DEATH.

THE GUY BEING SKEWERED IS THEIR KING FOR A YEAR. THE GUY DOING THE SKEWERING IS A BARD! THE KIT MARLOWE OF HIS TIME.

IN THIS SOCIETY BARDS ARE REVERED AS THE HOLIEST OF MEN - CAN YOU BELIEVE IT?

"THE KING'S BLOOD WILL BE COLLECTED AND SCATTERED ACROSS THE GROUND SO AS TO BRING REBIRTH -- THE GROWTH OF NEW CROPS, THE BUDDING OF NEW FLOWERS."

TROUBLE IS, OUR BARD FRIENDS GET A *TASTE* FOR SPILLING BLOOD. OVER THE MILLENNIA THEIR *INFLUENCE* SPREADS.

THEY ARE THE DEATH OF DARKEST WINTER, THE FLAME THAT ENABLES NEW LIFE TO FLOURISH.

THEY CAUSE THE DESTRUCTION OF BABYLON--

--THE DEATH OF OZYMANDIAS--

--THE DISSOLUTION OF CAMELOT--

--THE CRUSHING OF ATHENIAN DEMOCRACY IN THE PELOPONESIAN WAR--

--THE RISE OF GENOCIDAL DESPOTS--

--AND ON IT GOES.

PLOTTING THE TRAJECTORY OF THEIR 'ACHIEVEMENTS' LEADS TO GLOBAL ANNIHILATION BY THE YEAR 2020.

NONSENSE. HOW CAN A BAND OF PAGAN CUT THROATS DO THIS?

NOT CUTTHROATS, MARLOWE, THE GREATEST STORYTELLERS WHO EVER LIVED -- VISIONARIES, REVOLUTIONARIES, GIFTED WITH THE POWER TO TURN THEIR IMAGININGS INTO REALITY."

THEIR RULING COUNCIL INCLUDES FRIEDRICH NIETZSCHE AND JOSEPH CONRAD.

THOMAS MALLORY, MARY SHELLEY.

YOUR FAVOURITE 'ARSE HARLOT', SHAKESPEARE.

AND YOUR MENTOR, FRANCIS BACON.

HOW DO YOU KNOW THIS?

THE CLUES ARE IN THEIR WRITING. USING POWERFUL MACHINES CALLED COMPUTERS WE'VE DISCOVERED PATTERNS, LINKS, PHRASES, SHARED METAPHORS.

WE'VE FOUND THEY CAN TRAVEL AT WILL INTO THE COLLECTIVE UNCONSCIOUS.

WE BELIEVE THEY'VE CREATED A CITY THERE - CALLED *NEW ATLANTIS* BY BACON - WHERE BARDS FROM ACROSS THE MILLENNIA CONVENE AND CONSPIRE.

"I live six thousand feet beyond man and time."
Friedrich Nietzsche

"It was the secret of Heaven and Earth that I desired to learn."
Mary Shelley

"Not mine own fears, nor the prophetic soul Of the wide world dreaming on things to come."
William Shakespeare

Joseph Conrad

"OUR FOUNDATIONS ARE THE SECRET KNOWLEDGE OF THINGS, AND THE ENLARGING OF THE BOUNDS OF HUMAN EMPIRE, SO MAKING ALL THINGS POSSIBLE."
FRANCIS BACON

IT'S FROM HERE THEY'RE PLANNING TO UNLEASH ON OUR WORLD A TRULY DEVASTATING ATTACK--

--LITERALLY AN INVASION OF OUR *WORST NIGHTMARES.*

THEN *STOP* THEM.

AND HOW DO YOU SUGGEST WE DO THAT?

TRAVEL BACK IN TIME AND KILL THEM. DO TO THEM FIRST WHAT THEY WOULD DO.

SADLY IT'S NOT THAT EASY. RECOGNISE WHERE WE ARE?

NOW – COME DOWN AND JOIN US IN OUR HOME.

NO NEED TO KNOCK.

GREETINGS, HERR MARLOWE.

MY NAME IS *RICHARD WAGNER*. LET ME INTRODUCE YOU MY FAMILY.

LOGE, LORD OF FIRE AND MISCHIEF--

BRUNNHILDE, WARRIOR QUEEN, KEENING FOR THE BLOOD SPILT OF MORTAL MAN.

WOTAN – KING OF THE GODS--

--*SIEGFRIED* , NEVER BESTED BY MORTAL IN COMBAT--

--AND *ALBERICH* OF THE NIBELUNGEN.

I'VE EXPLAINED TO THEM THAT YOU'VE COME TO *STEAL* SOMETHING FROM THEM. SOMETHING *VERY PRECIOUS*. SO PRECIOUS INDEED THAT THEY'LL DO *WHATEVER IT TAKES* TO STOP YOU.

THE WOMAN LEAPS FORWARD, SCREACHING WITH A MIXTURE OF INDIGNATION AND FURY.

HER SPEARPOINT DARTS TOWARDS MY GUT--

--AS THE ONE WITH THE AXE CIRCLES BEHIND ME.

AND FROM SOMEWHERE COMES THE SOUND OF SINGING.

A CHOIR OF ANGELS REACHING FOR THE SUBLIME IN AN ASCENDING, WORDLESS ARPEGGIO--

--LIKE A CATARACT FALLING HEAVENWARDS.

UNTIL I REALISE IT IS *MY BLOOD* SINGING, *MY MUSCLES, MY TENDONS,* FLOWING IN AN *EFFORTLESS* CADENCE.

"THIS IS NO DREAM", HELEN SAID.

IF SHE SPOKE TRUE, IF I AM AWAKE NOW, THEN MY LIFE BEFORE WAS A DREAM.

HOW CAN THIS BE? I AM NO FIGHTER. MY SKIN IS SOFT, MY CHIN SPARSELY BRISTLED AND MY LIMBS AS WEAK AS A VEAL CALF'S.

OFT-TIMES HAVE I WONDERED IF I AM HALF-WOMAN.

YET NOW I DESPATCH THESE WARRIORS FROM ANTIQUITY AS CASUALLY AS CASTING ASIDE MY COAT.

THEIR MOVEMENTS ARE PONDEROUS, AND THEIR WEAPONS HAVE THE HEFT OF A CHILD'S PLAYTHINGS.

I DANCE ABOUT THEM AS IF I WERE A DERVISH FROM THE DARK CONTINENT AND THEIR BONES CRACK AND CRUMBLE IN MY HANDS.

WAGNER, I APPEAR TO HAVE EXHAUSTED YOUR FAMILY MEMBERS. HAVE YOU MORE RELATIVES FOR ME TO GREET?

NO WONDER THE BARDS FEAR YOU. THIS IS AN ALTOGETHER IMPRESSIVE DISPLAY.

BUT, YES, THERE IS ANOTHER. ALLOW ME TO INTRODUCE...

ENOUGH.

IF WHAT YOU SAY IS TRUE ALL OUR ENERGIES MUST BE DIVERTED TO APPREHENDING MARLOWE.

AND WHAT WHEN WE FIND HIM?

WE GRAB THE TIGER BY THE TAIL, NATURALLY, AND ASK HIM TO SURRENDER.

OUR SOLE CONSOLATION IS THAT MARLOWE IS NOT YET AWARE OF THE EXTENT OF HIS POWERS.

IF HE WERE, WE WOULD HAVE BEEN DESTROYED ALREADY.

MALLORY?

THE SIMILARITY IN OUR NAMES IS NO COINCIDENCE.

WE SHARE A CONNECTION IN BLOOD.

I SENSE HIM, FEEL HIS TENTATIVE FUMBLING TOWARD SELF AWARENESS.

WHILE YOU OLD MEN SIT HERE AND WRING YOUR HANDS I WILL HUNT HIM DOWN.

AND I SHALL DESTROY HIM!

His looks do menace heaven
and dare the Gods.
His fiery eyes are fixed upon the earth.

Christopher Marlowe

Chapter three
The Druid

WHAT JUST HAPPENED? WHAT THE *FUCKING* CHRIST WAS THAT THING?

WHERE IS HE?

WHY DIDN'T HE COME BACK WITH ME?

NEVER MIND THAT. YOU'RE GOING TO WANT TO LOOK AT *THIS*.

WE HAD A CAMERA ON HIM THE WHOLE TIME.

OK, WE'RE AT THE POINT ON THE SIMULATION WHERE THE *DRAGON* IS ABOUT TO SWALLOW HIM.

LOOK -- PURE *ID ENERGY*, BUT OF A MAGNITUDE *NEVER* ENCOUNTERED.

THOSE HELMETS ARE HIGH TRANSDUCTION CERAMIC.

THEY'LL ABSORB THE ENERGY GIVEN OFF BY A *CITY* WITHOUT GETTING WARM.

MARLOWE MANAGED TO MELT *HIS* INTO *SLAG* BEFORE HE VANISHED.

MY GOD.

MS WAL-SING-HAM, THE LIGHTS IN MY OFFICE FLICKERED A FEW MOMENTS AGO.

MIGHT THIS BE CONNECTED TO YOUR *EXPERIMENTS* ON MARLOWE?

WE'VE GATHERED SOME *STAGGERING* DATA ON OUR SUBJECT.

THEN *ILLUMINATE* ME. JOIN ME, PLEASE IN MY *EYRIE*.

I WANTED TO RECREATE THE CONDITIONS THAT BROUGHT HIM HERE SO TOOK HIM INTO A *SIMULATION*.

DID HE REALISE?

NO -- HE HAD TO BELIEVE THE JEOPARDY WAS *REAL*.

WE THINK IT WAS THE THREAT OF DEATH THAT TRIGGERED HIS INITIAL FLIGHT TO US. SO WE CREATED A SIMILAR THREAT.

AND THE RESULTS WERE *SPECTACULAR*.

THE RELEASE OF POWER WAS *ENORMOUS*. WE HAD TO RECALIBRATE OUR INSTRUMENTS TO A SCALE WE'VE *NEVER* GONE NEAR.

AND EVEN THEN IT THREATENED TO KNOCK OUT THE *ENTIRE* SYSTEM.

FASCINATING. WHAT IS THIS CREATURE

WE GUESS IT'S *THE GATEKEEPER* OF MARLOWE'S SUB-CONSCIOUS, A BEING FORMED OF *PURE ID ENERGY*

NO WONDER THE BARDS *FEAR* HIM. IT'S WORLDS BEYOND *ANYTHING* THEY'RE CAPABLE OF.

AND THE ENERGY SIGNATURE IS SO POWERFUL IT ACTS AS A *HOMING BEACON*.

WE'RE USING A TACHYON SCAN TO TRAWL FOR THE SIGNATURE. THE NEXT TIME HE USES IT WE'LL BE READY FOR HIM.

DON'T IMAGINE THE BARDS WILL BE IDLE, HELEN.

WE ARE IN A RACE. IF THEY WIN, IF THEY CAPTURE MARLOWE, IF THEY FIND A WAY OF TAPPING THIS ENERGY, THEN I *FEAR FOR OUR WORLD*.

LET'S HAVE SOME LIGHT IN HERE.

MS WAALSINGHAM, PLEASE MOVE YOUR HEAD TO ONE SIDE

AAIIEEEE - - EEEEIIAAARGH

THE NEMORENSIS

THE OLDEST OF ALL ARCHETYPES, THE MONSTER IN THE SHADOWS OF OUR NIGHTMARES, THE REAVER, THE SACRIFICING PRIEST.

IT MUST BE EVIL - - IT SMELLS OF BURNT CABBAGE.

DARE I ASK WHERE IT CAME FROM? DID YOU KILL IT?

WHAT SILLY QUESTIONS. CAN YOU KILL A DREAM?

AS TO ITS SOURCE -

THE NEMETON IS THE SACRED PLACE WHERE THE NEMORENSIS RESIDES AND THE BARDS ARE HIS DISCIPLES.

WE SEEM TO HAVE CAUGHT THEIR ATTENTION.

YEAH, THE WAY KICKING A HORNETS' NEST CAPTURES THEIR ATTENTION.

HOW DO YOU SUPPOSE THEY'RE LINKED TO MARLOWE?

IF THE MARKER HE LEFT IS AS EASY TO FOLLOW AS YOU SAY, WE SHALL BE SHORTLY FINDING OUT.

DRUIDS -- BAH, A CARTLOAD OF ARSEPUKE.
OH BARDS OF NEMETON -- HANG OAK-CROWNED HEADS AND PRAY.
THE BARDS. NEMETON. WHERE ARE THEY. ARE *YOU* ONE?
SPEAK YOU POX-FLECKED, MAGGOT-ADDLED, SHIT-SMEAR.
AH
OUR DOOM COMES ALMONG US!

HELEN, WAKE UP.

HHM -- JUST A FEW MINUTES MORE -- I FEEL SO *DREAMY*.

WAKE UP -- SOME PEOPLE WANT TO TALK TO YOU.

WAKE UP!!

OH MY --

ALL THIS *CRAP* ABOUT ENLIGHTENMENT AND RENEWAL.

WHAT I SEE IS THE PRODUCT OF A BUNCH OF *FUCKING PERVERTS*.

I'M PLEASED YOU'RE IN SUCH A *TALKATIVE MOOD*, MISS WALSINGHAM, SINCE WE'VE ONE OR TWO QUESTIONS WE'D LIKE YOU TO ANSWER.

WHY DON'T YOU COME DOWN AND TAKE A SEAT?

This soul should fly from me,
and I be changed
Unto some brutish beast
　　　　Christopher Marlowe

Chapter four
The Greenway

AH, HELEN - WELCOME BACK. I SENSE YOUR EXPEDITION WAS A *SUCCESSFUL* ONE?

THE BARDS WERE TRICKED INTO GIVING YOU THEIR ID ENERGY SIGNATURES?

AFFIRMATIVE. IT'S ALL STORED IN THE ARMOUR'S NEURAL NETWORK.

NOW TAKE IT *AWAY!* MAKE THEM GO!

THE SUIT DIDN'T PROTECT ME!

I'M AWAKE INSIDE THEIR *FEVER DREAMS!*

THIS PLACE IS LIKE BEING IN A DREAM.

I FEEL I'VE BEEN HERE BEFORE - MANY TIMES --

AS OF COURSE YOU *HAVE*, PLAYWRIGHT.

FOR THE GREENWAY IS YOUR MIND'S PHILOSOPHER'S STONE.

WHATEVER YOU DREAM THERE BECOMES YOUR REALITY.

IT IS THE *WILD WOOD.*

WILD WOOD - YOU LOON! CESSPIT MORE LIKE!

FROM THE SMELL OF IT YOUR DRUIDS HAVE BEEN EMPTYING *THEIR GUTS* IN THIS POOL FOR A THOUSAND YEARS.

SO QUICK TO *MOCK.* I WONDER WHAT THE NEMETON SEES IN YOU.

YET, SEE HERE, A SIGN OF FORTUNE - A CLUSTER OF ACORNS.

WEAR IT ON YOUR BREAST AS AN EMBLEM OF LUCK.

VERY WELL - ON CONDITION YOU SEAL YOU LIPS FOR A MINUTE OR TWO.

THE POOL'S AS BLACK OF NIGHT.

I'M TO ASSUME IT SYMBOLISES MY *GODLESS* SOUL?

OF COURSE.

THEN LETS SEE HOW *DEEP* THESE STILL WATERS RUN.

NO - NO STONES!

AH, YOU ARE IN ERROR - FOR NOW YOUR ONE REFLECTION IS MANY.

AND NOT *ALL* HAVE SUCH CHARMING DISPOSITIONS AS YOU...

LOOK BEHIND US - A SURFEIT OF MARLOWES.

THIS WAY - TO THE TREE TOPS IF YOU VALUE YOUR LIFE!

OUT OF THE WAY YOU WANG - SKULLED TURD PILE!

REMEMBER THE POOL - THE REFLECTIONS - ONE MAN AND MANY....

IMPERVIOUS TO WORDS, PERHAPS BUT NOT THE *MAN!*

YES - THE MANY....

MARLOWE THE PLAYWRIGHT.

MARLOWE, THE POET.

THE FIGHTER.

THE ATHEIST.

THE ARTIST.

THE RABBLE ROUSER.

MARLOWE, THE SPY... AND THE LOVER.

MARLOW THE LEGION!!!

I PASSED THE TEST - I LED MY WARRING SELVES TO VICTORY!

THE TEST WAS TO WORK AS ONE, NOT CREATE INDIVIDUAL DOMINANCE.

BOLLOCKS. I'LL NOT SURRENDER THE ESSENCE OF WHAT MAKES MARLOWE.

IT IS THIS VERY UNIQUENESS THAT INSPIRED MY INFERIOR COPIES TO FOLLOW.

INDEED? HMM - WHAT BECAME OF THE ACORN CLUSTER

DISLODGED IN THE MELEE

NAY, MARLOWE, ITS STILL AFFIXED.

SAVE THE ONE WEARING IT LIES HITHER, A SHARD THROUGH HIS HEART.

YES, THE "UNIQUE" MARLOWE WHO CLIMBED THE TREE WITH ME IS DEAD WHILE YOU IT SEEMS ARE AN "INFERIOR" COPY...

I FOUND THIS BROKEN MIRROR IN THE RUINS. LOOK IN IT.

THE INDIVIDUAL SELF IS AN ILLUSION MARLOWE.

LEARNING THIS TRUTH PASSES THE TEST - NOT KILLING A MONSTER.

NOW, LETS RETURN TO THE GREENWAY.

AND LOOK, YOUR COMPANION MASTER FRAZIER YET LIVES.

HE IS NO COMPANIION OF MINE - HE WOULD HAVE KILLED ME, GIVEN THE CHANCE --

-- KILLED ME OR KILLED ANOTHER? MY BRAIN RACES AS IF IN A FEVER....

FEVER? THEN YOU MUST COOL OFF!

NO!!!!!

AAARGH I CAN'T FUCKING SWIM!

BASTARD!

YOU PIGSHIT-BUBO SWATHED QUIM-MOUTHED FANNY-BREATHED SON OF SPUNK!!

I'LL TEAR YOUR EARS OFF AND USE THEM AS PIE CRUST TO BAKE YOUR BOLLOCKS IN!

YES, YES... THATS IT... FEEL IT COME OUT AND SAY WHAT YOU THINK.

PUT AWAY YOUR FANGS, HOUND!

AND SHOW ME WHO STANDS BEHIND YOUR MASK.

AHHH - CHRIST ALIVE! THIS HURTS! MAKE IT STOP!

WHOEVER YOU ARE - I HAVE NO PATIENCE FOR TEDIOUS QUESTIONS.

TELL ME ALL I NEED TO KNOW.

OR I WILL BURN YOU!

MY NAME IS SIR THOMAS MALLORY.

I AM A BARD.

I AM YOUR ASSASSIN.

I INHABITED FRAZIER'S BODY AND BROKE INTO THE INN - TO OBSERVE YOU - PROBE FOR WEAKNESSES - AND TO STRIKE WHEN THE TIME IS RIPE.

WHY MAN? NEVER HAVE I THREATENED THE BARDS. NOR WOULD I HAVE?

TO THE BARDS PAST AND FUTURE ARE ONE. WE SEE WHAT YOU BECOME.

SEE FOR YOURSELF...

YOU KNOW WHAT I SAY IS THE TRUTH

YOU KNOW TOO, WHAT YOU MUST DO

IT IS AS MERLIN SAYS -- PATTERNS EMERGE, PATHS CONVERGE, THERE IS ONLY ONE COURSE I CAN TAKE --

-- CHRISTOPHER MARLOWE MUST *DIE!*

IF WE DO THIS SHE MIGHT DIE.

THE FORCE OF THE BARDS' ASSAULT FUSED THE SUIT'S NEURAL LACE INTO HER NERVOUS SYSTEM.

DOWNLOADING THEIR ENERGY PATTERNS COULD *ERASE* HER MIND.

'MIGHT' -- 'COULD' -- I'M NOT INTERESTED IN YOUR *THEORIES*, CONTROL

THE ENERGY PATTERNS IN THE SUIT GIVE US THE ABILITY TO TAKE THE FIGHT TO THE BARDS, TO *FIGHT FIRE WITH FIRE.*

COMMENCE THE PROCEDURE.

VERY WELL.

THE BOOK - IT COMES TO LIFE BEFORE ME!

WRIGGLE IT AS MUCH AS YOU LIKE CHRISTTOPHER MARLOWE; I HAVE YOU TRAPPED IN ITS PAGES!

AND SOON WE WILL GIVE BIRTH TO A NEW PARADISE!

OH MY GOD! THE SWEET ORGASMIC BEAUTY OF IT!

Cut is the branch that might
   have grown full straight,
And burned is Apollo's laurel bough,
That sometimes grew
   within this learned man

      Christopher Marlowe

Chapter five:
The Umbilicus

AND NOW MY LIFE UNRAVELS LIKE THE STRANDS OF A FRAYED TAPESTRY. IN THIS STRAND I AM WAGING WAR.

MULTIPLE VERSIONS OF ME BLOOM IN THE MELEE.

I AM STRUCK, CUT DOWN, DARKNESS CLOSES AROUND ME.

THEN I AM ANOTHER - WHOLE VIBRANT, DEADLY.

I AM MARLOWE. I AM *LEGION*.

MY DOUBLES SURGE AROUND ME, GUARDING MY BACK, AS I GUARD THEIRS. EACH THE OWNER OF MY UNIQUE CONCIOUSNESS.

MY FOES RISE AS IMPOTENTLY AS A WAVE AGAINST A ROCK. THEY ARE CHAFF. THEY ARE FALLEN LEAVES, SKITTERED BY THE WIND.

THEY ARE *NOTHING*, PATHETIC DIVERSIONARY CLUTTER THROWN AT ME TO DISTRACT US FROM OUR REAL PREY, OUR TRUE ENEMY --

-- THE MAN WHO WOULD RAISE HIMSELF UP AS A *GOD* --

IN ANOTHER STRAND I MAKE LOVE.

THE VELVET FURROWS OF YOUR BACK BEWITCH AND CONFUSE.

YOU CAST A LINE OF SILVER GOSSAMER AND REELED ME IN ACROSS THE CENTURIES.

AND FOR THAT I OFFER YOU A PAYMENT.

A PAYMENT? OF WHAT?

A BEARER BOND, MY LADY. DRAWN ON MY HEART, MY BODY, MY SOUL.

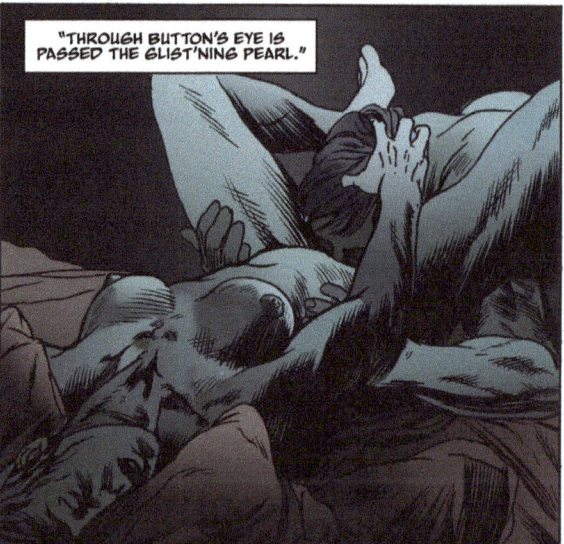

"THROUGH BUTTON'S EYE IS PASSED THE GLIST'NING PEARL."

"WEFTED THREADS ENTWINED ON BOBBINS BEAM."

"MAKE GATHERED CLEFTS OF VELVET KNOT UNFURL --"

" -- AND CLASP WITHIN THE CLOSURE'S HIDDEN SEAM. "

AND YET ANOTHER STRAND. THE BARD CALLED THOMAS MALLORY INSTRUCTS ME ON THE FINER ARTS OF SUICIDE.

"IN YOUR CURRENT STATE MARLOWE, YOU'RE ALL BUT INDESTRUCTIBLE."

"A LIFE FORCE COURSES THROUGH YOU THAT WILL *NOT* BE DENIED."

"IT WILL NOT PERMIT YOU - NOR ANYONE ELSE - TO TAKE YOUR LIFE."

"THEN HOW, MALLORY, AM I TO END MY LIFE?"

"SIMPLE. YOU MUST LOCATE YOURSELF AT A POINT IN YOUR FUTURE."

"AT A POINT WHEN YOUR FUTURE SELF HAS BEEN TESTED ALMOST BEYOND ENDURANCE, AT THE CLIMAX OF A DESPERATE BATTLE WITH MORTAL ENEMIES PERHAPS."

"A POINT WHEN YOUR POWERS OF YOUR FUTURE SELF ARE *EXHAUSTED*. WHEN YOUR RESISTANCE IS *BROKEN*."

"IT IS THERE, YOU MUST DELIVER THE *COUPE DE GRACE*."

AND SO WE COME TO WIPE AWAY THE SINS...

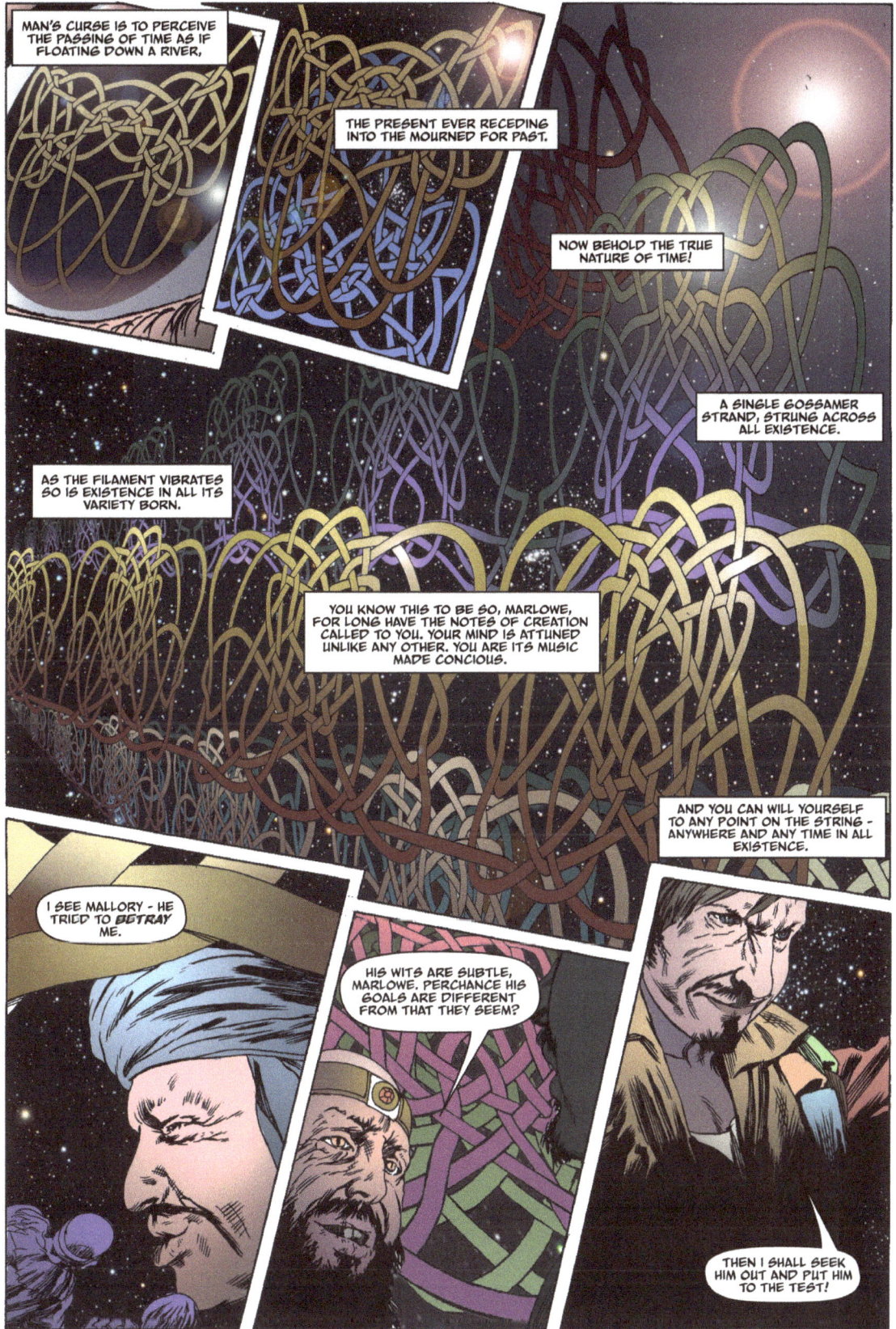

MARLOWE'S DEAD.

GOOD, THOMAS. HOW DID YOU DO IT?

HIS WEAKNESS IN HIS MORALITY. I PERSUADED HIM THAT THE WORLD IS BETTER WITHOUT HIM.

OF COURSE MARLOWE ISN'T ALONE IN THIS DISABILITY.

IN TRUTH, THERE ARE ONLY TWO UTTERLY FREE OF THAT CURSE. I AM ONE --

AND YOU, HERR JUNS, ARE THE OTHER.

SINCE BECOMING A BARD YOU STOKED OUR FEARS ABOUT THE FORCE FROM THE FUTURE. THE WALSINGHAM WOMAN FINDING AND USING MARLOWE TO DESTROY US.

YOU HAVE MADE US JUMP AT SHADOWS - BELIEVING SHAKESPEARE WAS A TRAITOR.

IT WAS OUR PROVOCATION THAT UNLEASHES THE VERY POWERS YOU WARNED US OF.

I WATCHED MARLOWE AT CLOSE QUARTERS AND HE WAS *NOT* THE MONSTER YOU PORTRAY.

POWERFUL, YES, BUT THREATENING ONLY BECAUSE WE THREATENED HIM.

THIS RED BOOK YOUR ALWAYS CARRY WITH YOU. GIVE IT TO ME.

NO - HAND IT BACK!

HAVE A CARE, OLD MAN. MY BEAST RAVENS.

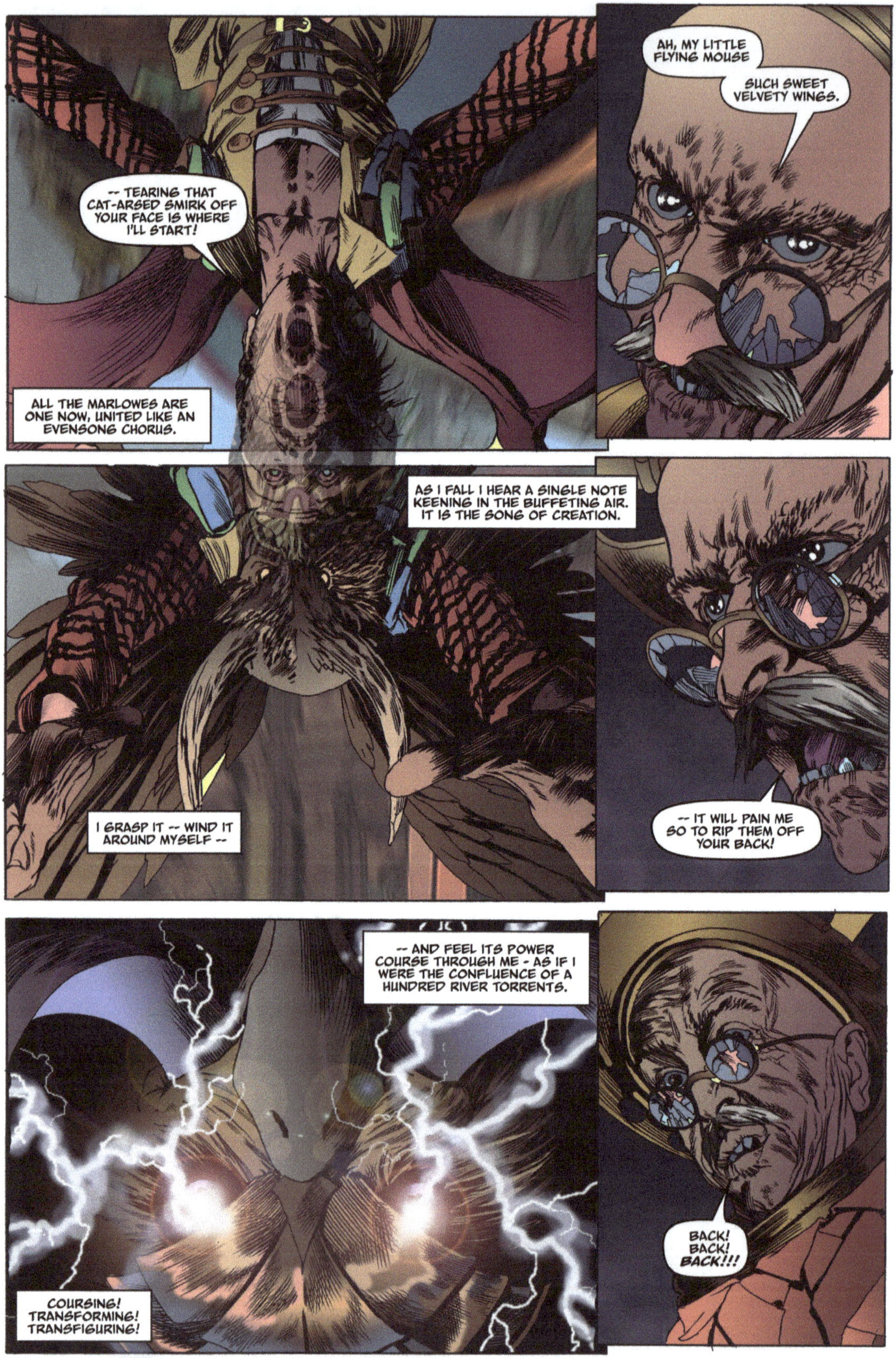

AH, MY LITTLE FLYING MOUSE

SUCH SWEET VELVETY WINGS.

-- TEARING THAT CAT-ARSED SMIRK OFF YOUR FACE IS WHERE I'LL START!

ALL THE MARLOWES ARE ONE NOW, UNITED LIKE AN EVENSONG CHORUS.

AS I FALL I HEAR A SINGLE NOTE KEENING IN THE BUFFETING AIR. IT IS THE SONG OF CREATION.

I GRASP IT -- WIND IT AROUND MYSELF --

-- IT WILL PAIN ME SO TO RIP THEM OFF YOUR BACK!

-- AND FEEL ITS POWER COURSE THROUGH ME - AS IF I WERE THE CONFLUENCE OF A HUNDRED RIVER TORRENTS.

BACK! BACK! BACK!!!

COURSING! TRANSFORMING! TRANSFIGURING!

EVERYTHING OCCLUDES ON THIS ONE POINT - CONCENTRATING INTO A SEETHING BOLUS TO SIZE OF A PINHEAD --

-- SILENCE LIKE AN IN-BREATH BEFORE THE PLUNGE.

THEN IT *EXPLODES*, THE SONG RUNNING THROUGH ME, LIQUID AND ELDRITCH, FASTER AND FASTER.

JUNG *SCREAMS* FOR MERCY --

-- VAPORISES.

A WAVE OF DESTRUCTION SWEEPS ACROSS THE CITY --

-- AND I AM LEFT, SPENT, EMPTY AND POWERLESS.

NOW - TELL ME TRUE - WHAT DO YOU THINK OF MY HANDIWORK?

-- I SEND YOU TO THE ETERNAL SLEEP.

A HEARTBEAT, A FLICKER OF CONSCIOUSNESS - I LIVE!

IT IS AS MERLIN SAYS : ALL STRANDS ARE BUT ONE, ENDLESSLY REPEATING, LEADING IN BUT ONE DIRECTION..

SOON NOW, MY BRAVE WARRIORS.

SOON SHALL YOU WALK IN GROVES OF MOONLIT CYPRESS.

WHERE ARE WE? WHO ARE YOU?

A SIMPLE FERRYMAN. CRADLING THE DEPARTED ON THEIR LAST, GREAT CROSSING

I ASK ONLY A MODEST PAYMENT - AN OBOL FROM THE MOUTH OF A DEAD MAN.

BEHOLD, OUR DESTINATION! NESTLED IN THE CONFLUENCE OF THE STYX AND ACHERON, THE GATEWAY TO...

WE HAVE NO SOULS, OLD MAN. WE TRAVEL ON A MISSION GREATER THAN YOUR PALTRY RECKONING.

YOU WILL *NOT* BE PAID!

INDEED?

FOOLHARDY WORDS. DO NOT THINK THAT THEY HAVE THE POWER TO SHAPE OUTCOMES.

FOR *THE DEAD* ARE NOT *ONLY* PASSENGERS....

SSSSSSS!

O, soul be changed into
little water drops
And fall into the ocean,
ne'er to be found

Christopher Marlowe

Chapter six:
The
Underworld

THE ISLAND ERUPTS LIKE A ROTTED CANINE TOOTH. OVERGROWN CYPRESSES AND DUSTY MAUSOLEUMS CLING TO ITS SIDES.

ABOVE THE MOORING POINT A GATE IS CARVED INTO THE VERY ROCK.

BUT NO LIVING PERSON EVER LANDS THERE.

I FULFIL MY PURPOSE CHRISTOPHER MARLOW. YOU ARE SAFE AND MAY CONTINUE ON YOUR JOURNEY.

I WILL PROTECT YOU ALWAYS.

I ASKED FOR PAYMENT. AND ALWAYS, I EXACT WHAT IS *OWED!*

RUN IF YOU MUST, LITTLE MAN.

CLING TO THOSE PRECIOUS LAST LUNGFULS OF AIR AND THAT FEARFUL RACING THOUGHT.

BUT, I *WILL* EXACT PAYMENT!

YOUR EFFORTS ARE ABSURD. THE *DEAD* OWE *ME* THEIR ALLIEGIANCE.

AND THIS IS A *NECROPOLIS!*

STAY STILL AND I SHALL MAKE YOUR PASSING SWIFT AND MERCIFUL!

IT ISN'T SUPPOSED TO BE LIKE THIS. I'VE SEEN OTHER THINGS – I HAVE A FUTURE!

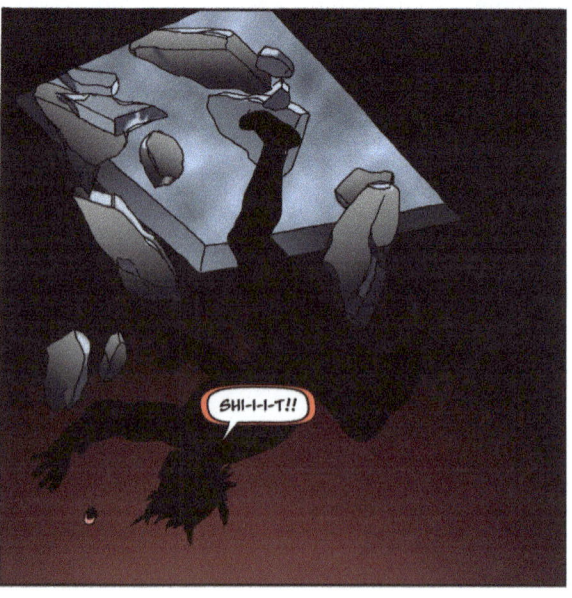

SHI-I-I-T!!

I DIDN'T SEE *THAT* COMING.

WHAT FRESH TORMENT IS THIS?

YOU THINK YOU HAVE ESCAPED?

THE PATH BELOW PROMISES ETERNAL TORMENT COMPARED TO THE DARK BLISS I OFFER!

RETURN AND I SHALL TREAT YOU MERCIFULLY.

YOUR MERCY? I'D SOONER HAVE A NETTLE POLTICE RUBBED ON MY ANUS!

DOWN I GO. WHEREVER IT MAY LEAD.

YES, DOWN. EACH ENCOUNTER HAS BEEN A STAGE ON MY DESCENT.

NOW POWERLESS I GO, INTO THE INFERNO.

'TIS LIKE A QUEST - FOR GRAIL OR GOLDEN FLEECE.

SAVE THAT I KNOW NOT WHAT MY SOUL IS.

AND I HAVE REACTED TO EVENTS...NEVER CAUSED THEM.

HAH, I HAVE BEEN A RUDE MECHANICALIS ANOTHER'S STORY.

WELL, NO MORE. IT IS TIME FOR MARLOWE TO TAKE *CENTRE STAGE.*

AH. HAH.

THIS MACHINE IS THE CONDUIT THROUGH WHICH I WILL SHORTLY TRANSFORM THE HUMAN RACE.

I HAVE SEEN YOU SO OFTEN IN MY VISIONS.

ALWAYS TO ONE SIDE - SCHEMING IN THE SHADOWS - WITH THE BARDS, BUT *NOT* ONE OF THEM.

THEIR FELLOWSHIP IS MAGNIFICENT. THEIR AIMS LOFTY AND INSPIRING. BUT THEY WERE SIMPLY A TOOL FOR GETTING ME TO WHERE I MOST WANTED TO BE.

AND WHERE WAS THAT?

WHY HERE, WITH YOU OF COURSE!

THIS IS THE OMPHALOS, CHRISTOPHER. THE EYE OF THE PSYCHIC NEEDLE. THE INTERSECTION BETWEEN LIGHT --

-- HEAVEN AND HELL --

-- CONSCIOUS AND SUB-CONCIOUS.

THE RED BOOK - IT HAS BEEN THERE FROM THE START, HASN'T IT?

I CALL IT MY *LIBER NOVUS*

IT CONTAINS ALL I HAVE LEARNT OF THE COLLECTIVE UNCONCIOUS. IT IS THIS MACHINES OPERATING SYSTEM.

'TIS PLAIN YOU WISH TO EXPLAIN YOURSELF. I BEG YOU, CHOOSE WORDS THIS SIMPLETON UNDERSTANDS.

WHAT DOES EDEN SYMBOLISE, MARLOWE?

INNOCENCE. PURITY. THE PERIL OF TEMPTATION.

WRONG. THE TRUTH IS FOUND DEEP IN THE GNOSTIC TEXTS. EDEN IS GOD HIMSELF.

WE WERE EXPELLED FROM EDEN IN THE SAME WAY THAT SHRAPNEL IS EXPELLED FROM AN EXPLOSION.

YES, GOD EXPLODED!

AND THE SOUL OF EACH AND EVERY HUMAN WHO EVER LIVED IS A TINY FRAGMENT OF GOD'S ESSENCE. OUR MADNESS IS BORN OF THIS TRAUMA.

WITH DIAMOND CLARITY I UNDERSTOOD MY MISSION. I WAS TO BE THE AGENT OF *INVOLUTION*. I WAS TO UNITE EACH OF THESE SHARDS. TO BE THE MID-WIFE TO GOD'S RE-BIRTH AND MAN'S SALVATION.

I HAD DISCOVERED THE EXISTENCE OF THE BARDS IN THE SAME TEXTS.

NOW I SOUGHT THEM OUT AND BECAME ONE OF THEM. THROUGH THEM I EXPLORED THE COLLECTIVE UNCONSCIOUS - THE SHARED 'UNDERMIND' OF MANKIND.

I RETURNED FROM MY GNOSTIC RETREAT TO THIS WORLD A MAN *REBORN*.

I WOULD USE THE UNDERMIND LIKE A CIRCUIT, UNIFYING EVERY HUMAN SOUL THAT HAS EVER EXISTED, COLLAPSING THEM INTO A SINGLE MOVEMENT IN TIME. PUTTING THE FRAGMENTS BACK TOGETHER.

THE PLAN WAS LONG IN GESTATION. I SLOWLY BUILT THE ORGANISATION THAT WOULD PROVIDE THE TECHNOLOGY TO POWER THE INVOLUTION WITH SATISFYING SIMPLICITY IT ALSO KEPT THE BARDS OFF MY SCENT BY THREATENING THEIR EXISTENCE.

THE FINAL COMPONENT WAS YOU, THE LAST LINE OF *MERLIN!*

AAAHHH - CAN YOU FEEL IT? THE LOOSENING, THE BLURRING?

IT STARTS WITH THE MEREST RIPPLE - WITH A SINGLE INDIVIDUAL HUMAN.

THEIR ESSENCE - THEIR SOUL IS STREWN ACROSS ALL OF SPACE AND TIME. THE FIRST OF BILLIONS.

NOOOO! THIS WILL NOT STAND!

SO - THE FINAL BATTLE.

YES IT MUST BE. THE SYMBOLISM IS DEMANDED.

WE ARE ENGORGED BOTH OF US, BY THE ID ENERGY IN THIS PLACE.

IT SWAMPS US, CHANGES OUR FORMS, IMBUES US WITH THE POWER OF TITANS.

BUT FOR AS LONG AS THE BOOK IS MINE, YOU ARE THE FLY AND I AM THE SWATTER.

YOUR BUZZING IRRITATES ME. IT IS DISTRACTING.

YET THE INVOLUTION CONTINUES...

A RIPPLE BECOMES A WAVE, A WAVE BECOMES A TSUNAMI.

SOULS ARE CONSUMED LIKE COAL IN A FURNACE.

AND GOD STIRS IN HIS GRAVE.

THE LAST PAGE - IT'S NOT THERE! WHERE IS IT? WHAT HAVE YOU DONE?

WHAT HAVE YOU DONE?

DONE? NOTHING REALLY. JUST DANCED.

OH - AND GONE ON A TRIP WHILE YOUR ATTENTION WAS ON OUR DANCING.

NOWHERE FAR. NOWHERE AT ALL, REALLY.

WE THOUGHT THE TEXT NEEDED *EDITING.*

NO!!! IT WILL CREATE A --

-- SHORT CIRCUIT...!

THE SAME THING ON EVERY PAGE.

OF COURSE. WHAT *ELSE* COULD IT BE?

JUNG GLIMPSED WHAT YOU KNOW. ALL OUR ACTIONS REPEAT ON A LOOP TO INFINITY.

NOT *MINE*. I CHOOSE TO STEP OFF THE LOOP. *FAREWELL* WIZARD.

FAREWELL MARLOWE.

UNTIL *NEXT* TIME.

DEPTFORD, LONDON - 30TH MAY 1593

I KNOW NOW TIME IS A *FALLACY*. EACH OF US IS A FLAME THAT BURNS FOR ETERNITY.

I HAVE NO ENEMIES - ANY WHO WISHES TO BATHE IN THE LIGHT I CAST IS *WELCOME*.

I FEAR *NO SHADOWS* BECAUSE I ILLUMINATE THE *DARKEST* CORNER.

WHAT SAY *YOU* --

HERMAPHRODITOS?

ONLY AN ETERNITY YOU SAY?

IF THAT'S ALL THE TIME WE HAVE, STOP TALKING, GET YOUR KIT OFF AND GET OVER HERE!

FOR SARAH.

Sweet Helen,
      make me immortal with a kiss!
Her lips suck forth my soul;
      see, where it flies!

                    Christopher Marlowe

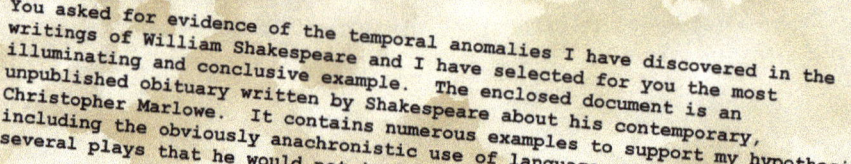

Magdalene College
Cambridge

ᵗʰ April 1934

dear professor,

You asked for evidence of the temporal anomalies I have discovered in the
writings of William Shakespeare and I have selected for you the most
illuminating and conclusive example. The enclosed document is an
unpublished obituary written by Shakespeare about his contemporary,
Christopher Marlowe. It contains numerous examples to support my hypothesis
including the obviously anachronistic use of language, and the reference to
several plays that he would not in fact write for some decades.

Most conclusive of all is the date: May 14th, 1593, some two weeks before
Marlowe's murder. You will point to the obituarist's common practise of
preparing his article before the subject's death. I will point you to the
reference in the obituary as to HOW Marlowe died.

'Thou Icarus: thy life to me is sweet'

— Me.

It is with profound shock and sadness that I
sit here to commemorate my great friend
Christopher Marlowe. My sadness is
inexpressible. I shall, however, bravely
write, hoping that my humble hand can
epitomise the spirit of my good friend Kit.

Some say he was an enigma but I would say
that would be to overstate it. He was in fact
very easy to understand. Some spoke of him
as a man of deep thought while I feel he was,
while not shallow, elegantly simple. He was
a simple man of simple pleasures. A good
fight, a glass of something strong, the love of
a good person; this was the Marlowe I knew;
a spontaneous, lovely, simple man.

Some might say that he was pompous,
patronising, selfish, megalomaniacal and
boorish. Not me. I know he was a gentle
and kind man, when he wasn't knocking the
teeth out of the nearest reveller at his
favourite pub. He was a generous man when
he wasn't cavorting with his Cambridge
contemporaries. Most pertinently, would a
man so megalomaniacal ask so much help of
his friend with his work? I think not.

No one will be surprised that Marlowe and I
saw one another as brethren. I was the older
brother. He would often come to me in fits
of literary insecurity saying, 'William I am
not good enough, I cannot finish this play.'

I would gently calm him down and help him
complete his work. Christopher Marlowe,
you may be surprised to hear, was in fact an
incredibly prolific writer; the quality of his
output frequently precluded publication. It
would fall upon me to help steer him away
from some of his most ludicrous ideas. One
such ludicrous inconsequential gem was a
fantasy in which a magician and his
daughter live on an island with a goblin and
a fairy and are attacked by pirates (or
something to this effect). Needless to say I
could not even finish said piece but of course
this is the life of the average writer; one in
which one must wade through the vast
quantities of waste in search of the few
buried diamonds. Through my assistance in
helping apply a quality control to Marlowe's
output I have accumulated a library of over
thirty discarded plays and this considerable
memento of the great man shall be a prize
cherished for the rest of my life.

It is hard for me to attest as to whether
Christopher Marlowe, as is so oft said, was
truly a godless man. He was definitely not a
God fearing man and would in fact often
mock me for being as I am, terrified of God.
In my humble opinion, he felt towards God
the way one may feel towards a lover who
had once scorned and humiliated them. I
know not what brought him to this point of
resentment but I feel that we should pay
sympathy not revulsion towards a man so
spiritually cuckolded.

We have all at some point in our lives felt such bitterness; he simply felt it on a grander scale. I would sit down sometimes to pray in his company and I would ask, 'do you want to sit with me and pray to our Lord God?' and although he would invariably tell me to, 'stop being such a child William' and that, 'God is but smoke and mirrors embraced only by the weak and ignorant' I could tell that part of him longed to embrace our great and terrifying lord. Every time he screamed 'I denounce God and all his works' he almost definitely was trying to say 'I love God and am a pious Christian'.

If he does, God forbid, now reside in hell then I am at least assured that he is burning with the best and brightest that hell has to offer. In the most sought after pool, next to the most exclusive dock of the most sulphurous lake of fire, that is where my Marlowe will eternally suffer. When I humbly ascend from this mortal coil one of the pleasures I await most feverishly is to wave down to Marlowe as a figure of solace through his struggle. Of course this is but negative and perhaps over-prudent thinking, but it is reckless not to have thought through contingencies.

It was no real secret that his voracious appetites extended to his bedroom (or whatever floor the dog saw as good enough). Marlowe was a man who did not discriminate when it came to sex and indeed there were many references to this inclination throughout his work. My suspicion has long been that the inclusion of Neptune as a character of ambiguous sexuality in 'Hero and Leander' was derived from his own nickname among his friends in Amsterdam as 'Christopher Marlowe – King of the Bath houses'. I don't think there was one among us in Marlowe's inner circle who had at one point not humorously quoted the man himself crying, 'You are deceived I am no woman' when he had a few too many.

How we would laugh. These occurrences should not be objects of ridicule but rather seen as evidence that he was a man who loved almost everyone he knew (in spite of the various accounts of his violent behaviour and of course the manner of his death).

He was not perturbed by boundaries of gender and would pursue his heart where he felt it and to this I commend him. I will however take this opportunity to reassert that I have not in fact pursued any homosexual activities myself in my time. Not with Kit and not with anyone. These are vicious and unfounded rumours. They are not true. I will repeat not true.

And so I bid farewell to you my dear Icarus. You flew so beautifully before you fell so incompetently. In many ways I feel he died as he probably would have wanted to go; right in the midst of a brawl with a knife through his eye, but his sudden passing still greatly hurts me. In a personal, perhaps ever so slightly selfish, way, I shall miss the presence of someone who supports and trusts me implicitly. The Patroclus to my Achilles. I shall miss the late nights back to back, furiously scribbling out the contents of our great minds. The ever so slight atmosphere of competition inspiring me to new and even greater heights of literary success.

I shall miss his familiar voice over my shoulder quietly asking me how to spell this or that word, advice on how to end this or that couplet. Our mutual body of great works will be left to speak for itself. My Titus Andronicus, Romeo and Juliet, Hamlet, Macbeth and King Lear. His Dr Faustus. These plays will live on as a lasting testament throughout the ages to our friendship. Shakespeare and his friend little Kit Marlowe. I hope right down at the base of my heart that if he is looking down (or up) on me now, he knows that I truly did learn from him in the same way he learned so very, very much from me.

It would be perhaps impudent to the church and the various societal bodies that Kit managed to offend and ostracise himself from (intentionally or not so), to not acknowledge that perhaps he got his just desserts. I would prefer to think of it as simply a premature lunch.

Did he in some sad way get what he deserved? Maybe. Was it right for his life to be taken as it was? Who could really say? However harshly the rest of history may remember him at least *I* know that he was a footnote more interesting than the paragraph he corresponded to, a magnificent candle amongst torches, the beautiful runt of the litter; a truly special man. Although history may well try to forget you, I will not dear friend. Your legacy will live on through me. At the very least people will read your name the world over in the appendices of my work. May you rest in peace or at least suffer in silence little flower. Too delicate for this world I shall bravely fight on for the both of us.

Your friend.
Your brother.
Your Shepherd through a world too complex and furious for you to comprehend.

William Shakespeare

Professor Jung, I cannot begin to express my gratitude for the interest and concern that you shown for me and this essential work. I risk professional censure and it affords me immense relief to know that I am supported by a figure of such renown and authority. I greatly look forward to visiting your sanatorium in Zurich during the summer.

Yours sincerely,
Daisy Bacon

Daisy Bacon was incarcerated in the Rheinhof Asylum for the Criminally Insane in June 1934 - an institution for which Doctor Jung was a visiting consultant. She was never released and died in September 1939.

Materials discovered by Gabriel Jones in the Rheinhof archive files

CHRISTOPHER MARLOWE AND THE BARDS OF NEMETON

Behind the foliage:
Origins, production sketches
and photoshop madness